NICOLA O'BYRNE

WHAT'S NEXT DOOR?

nosy crow

An imprint of Candlewick Press

Hey!

Where are we?

I can't see a thing in here.

Can anybody hear me?

If you're out there,

clap your hands

to **turn on** the light!

Thank you. That's **much** better.
But who's this?

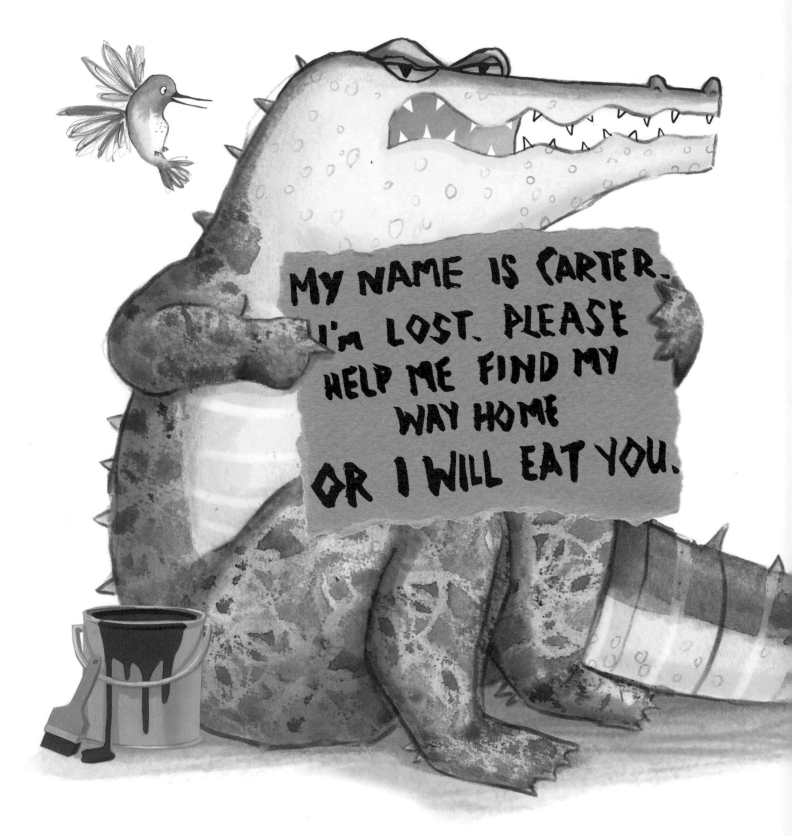

Hey! There'll be no **eating** in **this** book!
Let's help Carter get home.
How can we do that?

I know!
Let's **draw** a door!
Crocodiles like water,
so use your finger to **trace**
the dotted line and
think very hard about
somewhere **wet.**

Well done!
That's a **great** door!

But—oh, dear—it looks as if
it's a bit of a **squeeze** for Carter.

Can you **jiggle** and **wiggle** the book
to help him through?

Let's see what's next door. . . .

Oh, no! This can't be the right place.

Crocodiles like water,
but this sea is **far** too **stormy**.
Poor Carter!

Quick!
Use your finger
again and **draw** a circle.
We need a drain before
Carter gets seasick!

Well, that's better, but Carter's soaked through. Can you **blow** on him to dry him off? That might cheer him up a bit.

Let's try again. We need somewhere less stormy.

Draw a door with your finger and, whatever you do, don't think of the ocean!

That's a **very good** door,
but crocodiles have **big bottoms.**

Can you **tip** the book to help him fit through?

Let's see what's next door. . . .

Uh-oh! This isn't the right place
for Carter, either—it's **far** too **cold.**

Look at poor Carter. He's shivering!

Let's try to get rid of the snow.
Can you **turn** the book upside down
and **shake** the snow out?

Whoops! We made a blizzard instead.
And Carter looks really **unhappy.**
I do hope he isn't going to eat us.
Let's **rub** his tummy to warm him up.
That might help.

OK, let's get it right this time.

Think of somewhere **hot**.
Super **hot**.
Extra **hot**.
Ready?
Use your finger
to **draw**
a door.

Good work!
Just look at that door!

Do you think Carter
will fit through it?
Can you give him
a big **push**?

Let's see what's next door. . . .

Ooh, it's SO warm here.
Just perfect.

But . . . what's wrong now?
Do you think it's too
hot for Carter?

Yep, it's definitely too **hot!**
Look, Carter had to lie down.

Quick! **Fan** him with your hand!

So, we need a place that's not too **dark**,
not too **stormy**, not too **cold**,
and not too **hot**.

We need
another door!

Use your finger to trace the line and **think** very hard about somewhere that's **just right.**

Great!

Here we go again!

Let's see what's next door. . . .

At last! Carter's home!
He looks very **happy**, doesn't he?

But it's not home for everyone.
Where did these other **animals** come from?

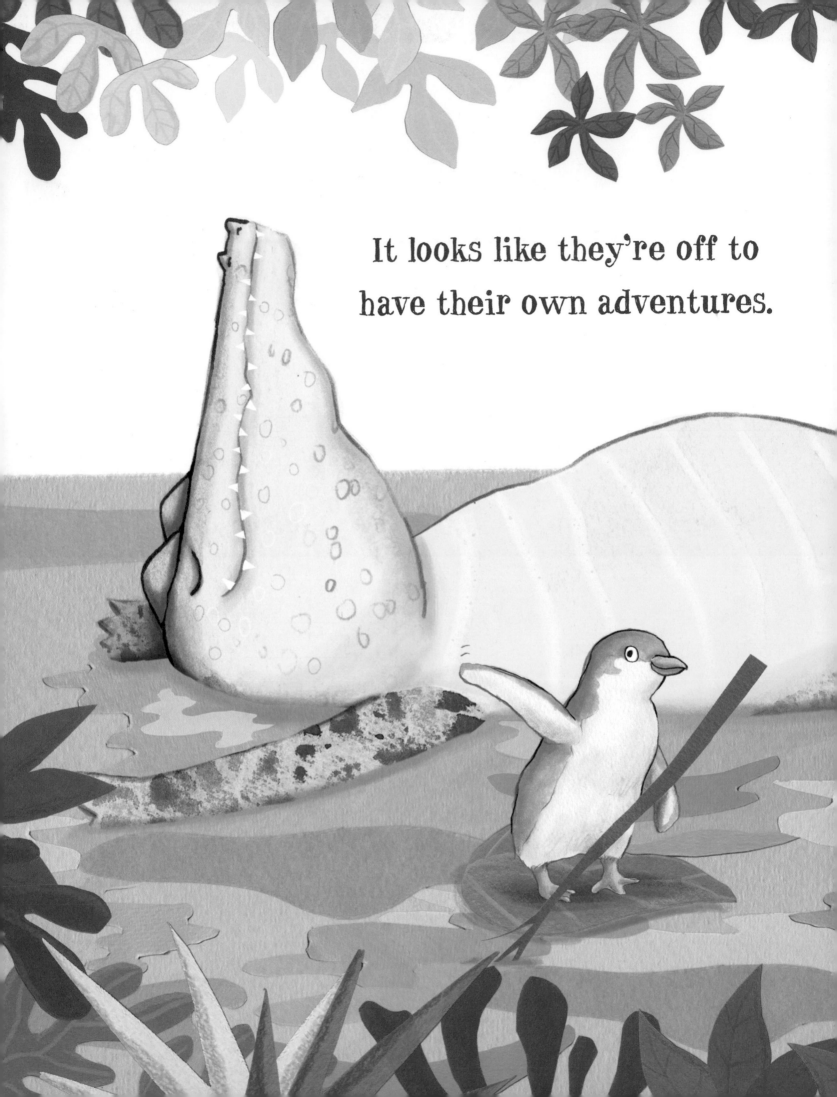

It looks like they're off to have their own adventures.